*f*ocus, B.

George. La Zebra. George. La Zebra.

B took a deep breath.

"T-R-A-N-S-F-O-R-M."

She cracked open an eyelid.

"Ohhhh . . . I can feel something happening!" George cried, patting his forehead. "It tingles! It . . . *huh*?"

He patted his scalp, just like when he was imitating the vice principal. Except, unlike the vice principal, George now had a tall, pointy, pink-lined set of ears on top of his head.

Covered with zebra stripes.

DISCOVER ALL THE MAGIC!

Spelling B

And the Runaway Spell

By Lexi Connor

SCHOLASTIC INC.

New York   Toronto   London   Auckland
Sydney   Mexico City   New Delhi   Hong Kong

No part of this publication may be reproduced, stored in a retrieval system, or transmitted in any form or by any means, electronic, mechanical, photocopying, recording, or otherwise, without written permission of the publisher. For information regarding permission, write to Working Partners Limited, Stanley House, St. Chad's Place, London WC1X 9HH, United Kingdom.

ISBN: 978-0-545-11738-8

Copyright © 2010 by Working Partners Ltd.
Series created by Working Partners Ltd., London
All rights reserved. Published by Scholastic Inc.,
557 Broadway, New York, NY 10012.
SCHOLASTIC, APPLE PAPERBACKS, and associated logos are trademarks and/or registered trademarks of Scholastic Inc.

12 11 10 9 8 7 6 5 4 3 2 1   10 11 12 13 14 15/0

Printed in the U.S.A.
First printing, January 2010

Special thanks to Julie Berry

To Joseph

Chapter 1

"Let me get this straight, B," George said, bouncing his soccer ball on his forehead. "All you have to do is spell a word, just some old random word, and you can make *anything* happen?"

Beatrix, "B" to her friends, flopped into the beanbag chair on her best friend's basement rec room floor. "It's not that simple, George," she said. "Watch out! You nearly hit the lamp."

George caught the ball. His thick, curly blond hair dangled over the rim of his glasses, but B could see the curiosity sparkling in his eyes. "W-I-N-D," she spelled, and a little breeze swept through the room, riffling her friend's hair.

George touched his forehead in amazement. "You really did that, didn't you? I still can't believe it." He began pacing back and forth. "So," he said, waving his hands wildly, "*so*, you could just spell 'win' and *bam*, our team could win the championship soccer game on Thursday? Just like that?" He wiggled his fingers.

B laughed. "No, I couldn't. And I wouldn't do a thing like that, even if I could."

Clearly, George didn't understand magic yet. And why should he? It was all so new to him. She hadn't meant to tell him she was a witch — he had discovered her secret by accident. All the same, it was a relief not to have to hide it from him anymore, and to have someone to talk to about her magic. She tried to explain herself better.

"Just because it's magic, George, doesn't mean it's like the movies. Real magic takes training and lots of practice. There are rules! Even still, things have a way of going wrong." She held up her hands, and George tossed her the ball. "Believe me, I know."

She tried bouncing the ball on her forehead, but

it got away from her and rolled across the broad room. George's huge yellow dog, Butterbrains, bounded after it.

"Show me another trick," George begged. "C'mon. One teensy little trick."

"They're not *tricks*," B said indignantly. "I'm not some circus performer. This is real."

"I know. Just one little . . . demonstration?"

"*Allllll* right," she said. "What do you want to see?"

George pointed at a lava lamp. "Make it, I dunno, float in the air or something." He fidgeted with excitement.

B focused on the lamp. "F-L-O-A-T," she said.

The lamp rose in the air and swung in a wide circle, as far as the power cord would let it travel. Butterbrains backed into a corner, his head cocked to one side. Now and then he gave a curious whimper, his tail thumping.

George crawled over to Butterbrains and tussled with him. "It's okay, boy! It's only B, the magic witch." He giggled. "This is just so stinking cool! I can't believe it. I can't *believe* it!"

B smiled. When George was excited about something, he had a one-track mind. *How long,* B wondered, *will it take him to get used to my magic?* She'd had a lifetime, growing up with parents and an older sister who were witches. True, their spells, like most other witches', were conjured by imaginative rhyming couplets, and not by spelling. Even so, minor magic such as floating objects had been commonplace in B's home for as long as she could remember.

Why not give him a little crash course?

"F-L-O-A-T," she whispered, concentrating on a plastic tote full of Wiffle balls and squooshy footballs. They slipped into the air silently and orbited over George's head.

"Whoa!" George paused his game with Butterbrains. "Lookit that!"

Butterbrains barked and jumped in the air, his body twisting as he tried in vain to snag the flying balls.

"D-A-N-C-E," B told a tub full of old, forgotten action figures George had long since outgrown.

Soon military figures were waltzing with monsters, and Greek heroes were tangoing with robots.

If George hung his mouth open any wider, he'd start drooling.

This was too much fun.

"B-U-I-L-D," she told a huge crate of interlocking blocks, and, clickety-clack, they flew out by the dozens to form themselves into a rainbow-colored replica of George's house, right down to the shrubs.

And still the lava lamp swung its wide arc, illuminating the bizarre party like a strobe light, while Butterbrains barked like a maniac.

"Oh, man," George said. "Think what you could do with this — the stuff you could pull off at school!" He doubled over laughing. "Just imagine, a school assembly, and you make the vice principal's toupee float all over the auditorium. *Attack of the bad hair monster!*"

B giggled. "No way! That's so mean. Besides, my magic is an absolute secret, remember? *No one* can find out about it."

"I know, I know," George said, still laughing. "You've gotta admit, though, that would be an assembly to remember." He pantomimed clutching at his head, as if his own hair had just flown away.

"Yeah, but you make me nervous, the way you keep bringing up ideas like that," B said, watching as the clackety building blocks turned George's house into a castle. "I would get in such huge trouble if the M.R.S. found out that you know about this."

"The what?" George asked.

"The Magical Rhyming Society."

George sat up, blinking at B. "There's a Magical Rhyming *Society*? You mean, there are lots of witches, all organized and stuff?"

"Yup. Lots of them." B aimed a G-L-O-W spell at a pair of glow-in-the-dark plastic swords. "What, did you think I'm the only one?"

Butterbrains ran in frenetic circles, barking at the bobbling balls, dancing figures, clashing swords, and building blocks, each in turn.

George shrugged. "How would I know? You're the only witch I've ever —"

KNOCK.

They stared at each other, terrified.

KNOCK.

They stared at the whirlwind of toys.

George's dad's voice came through the thin door.

"What are you two doing to that dog?"

Chapter 2

"D-R-O-P!" B whispered.

All the floating toys clattered to the floor. Just in time, George dived to catch the lava lamp before it smashed to bits.

George's dad poked his head through the door. "What on earth is going on in here?" He blinked at the sight of the toys all over the floor, then rolled his eyes. "Do I dare ask?"

B, her heart still pounding in her chest, let slip a nervous giggle. "We were just, you know, playing, Mr. F," she said.

Mr. Fitzsimmons rolled his eyes. "That's what toys are for, I guess. Clean this up, okay? And quit tormenting poor Butterbrains." He turned to go, then paused. "Oh, by the way. I came down here to tell you we just ordered some Chinese food. Should be here in a few minutes. Stick around for some Crab Rangoon, B?"

"Yum! You bet," B said. "Thanks for the invite."

George's dad nodded and pulled the door shut behind him as he went back upstairs.

"C'mon, George," B said, scooping up a handful of blocks. "Let's get this cleaned up."

"Can't you just think up a spell to do the cleaning?" George said.

B chucked a green brick at him. "Get cleaning, lazy. Spells are harder than you think. And they don't solve all your problems."

George dumped the action figures back in the tub. "Well, anyway, you were just about to tell me who the other witches are in our school."

B dropped an armload of balls into their tote. "I was not!"

"Oh, come on. Just whisper it to me. I won't tell," George teased.

B folded her arms across her chest. "No. Way. I've told you too much as it is. You might slip up and blab."

"Who, me?" He flung the plastic swords back into the toy box. "My lips are sealed."

"Good. Keep 'em that way. It would be a total disaster if any other nonwitches found out about me — or if any witches found out that I told you."

"I promise, B," George said seriously. "I won't let it slip."

B knew she could trust her best friend, but she was going to have to be really careful from now on. No more magic accidents!

"Um, B?" George said when they had almost finished cleaning up. "I've got a favor to ask you."

B sat back down in the beanbag chair and scratched Butterbrains's ribs with her toes. "What's up?"

George sat on the couch opposite her. He gestured to his shirt, on which a silk-screened soccer player with a streak of white hair was racing toward an invisible goal. "I've told you about Sergio Vavoso, right?"

"The, uh, Italian zebra?" B asked.

George beamed. "That's right. *La Zebra Italiana*, because of the stripe in his hair. The best soccer player ever in the whole world."

Of course B knew about the soccer player. George had been wearing his La Zebra sweatshirt every day since the weather had gotten cooler.

"What about him?"

"I know you can't do everything with magic." George bounced on the couch cushion. "But could you . . . could you . . . turn me into him?"

B slipped off the vinyl beanbag and landed on the floor. "Turn you into an international soccer star?"

George bit his lip. "Yeah. Then I'd be the most unstoppable soccer player in the whole league. The championship game would be no sweat!"

"You don't want me to try that," B said, picking herself up and sitting back on the beanbag. "It's, like, the magical equivalent of, I dunno, surgery. And I have trouble with the simplest spells."

George had started bouncing his soccer ball on his forehead. "Come on, B," he pleaded. "You don't have to *literally* turn me *into* him . . . just make me a little more like him. You know?"

She shook her head firmly. "I'm not ready for that kind of magic."

George gazed at B. His sad-eyed look could be more pathetic than Butterbrains's. "You can do it, B! You're amazing. Look at all you can do!" He gestured to the toys.

B waved away the compliments, but her friend persisted.

"This Thursday is the championship match. We can't lose! And I've been off my game lately, even Coach is saying so. I've got to turn it around or he may bench me. How would it look for the team captain to be sitting on the bench?"

B drummed her fingertips on her knees, thinking hard. Poor George! Was there some way she could help him? Oh, but it was risky. Did she dare try?

"I just need a little taste of what it's like to be him. Then I'll be ready for Spirit Week and be able to get psyched for the championship game."

B knew she could do some temporary spells, like a bag-cauldron spell. She'd never done one on her own before, but maybe she could try it?

She got up and began foraging around the basement, looking for things.

"Whatcha doing?" George asked, following her.

"Thinking." She found an empty shopping bag and set it on the floor. By the door to the garage, she found George's cap that had the Italian soccer team's crest embroidered on it. *That'll be perfect for my spell*, she thought. She scratched her head, then marched into Mrs. Fitzsimmons's basement laundry room, rummaged through a basket of dirty clothes, and pulled out one of George's long, orange, smelly soccer socks.

"Pee-yew!"

"Come on," George said. "Tell me what you're doing!"

B put her hands on her hips. "Be patient! I'm figuring out my spell."

"Wahoo!" George said, doing a happy dance.

"I'm going to try a bag-cauldron concoction. Have you got a picture of this Zebra guy of yours?"

George pulled a pack of sports trading cards out of his back pocket. "A bag *what*?"

"A bag-cauldron concoction is a little bit like a potion — it's a spell you make by mixing things. You make potions in a real cauldron, then you drink the brew, but bag-cauldron concoctions just produce the magic. There's nothing to drink. And you can assemble them in almost any container. A bag, a purse. I'm using this shopping bag. Make sense?"

George polished his glasses on his sweatshirt. "I guess so." He handed B a trading card. "Here it is. Limited edition Sergio Vavoso, extremely rare," he said. "Will I get it back?"

"I'm not sure. And I don't think the results will last long. Still want to do this?"

George hesitated, then nodded.

"Okay, then," she said. "Have a seat."

"Hey, I was going to wear that hat to school tomorrow for Crazy Hat Day," George protested. "I need as much spirit from Spirit Week as I can get!"

"Well, you'll need to find a crazier one," B said. "I need this one for the spell."

B tried not to let it show that she'd never done a bag-cauldron concoction before. Potions, yes, but this was different. Then again, what harm could it do to try? When her sister Dawn's friends had done bag-cauldron makeovers, the effects had only lasted a few seconds.

She placed the soccer and Zebra objects one by one into the shopping bag. She looked at George, waiting expectantly on the couch, then at the player on his shirt. She closed her eyes and tried to think about them both. A stray thought tickled her mind — *what if the Zebra turned into George, instead of the other way around*?

Focus, B.

George. La Zebra. George. La Zebra.

B took a deep breath.

"T-R-A-N-S-F-O-R-M."

She cracked open an eyelid.

"Ohhhh . . . I can feel something happening!" George cried, patting his forehead. "It tingles! It . . . *huh*?"

He patted his scalp, just like when he was imitating the vice principal. Except, unlike the vice principal, George now had a tall, pointy, pink-lined set of ears on top of his head.

Covered with zebra stripes.

Chapter 3

"Get these off me!"

B rolled on her back, laughing. "You asked for it, George! You wanted to be the Zebra; you got it."

"All right, all right, you had your little joke," George said. "Now make the ears go away."

B sat up, wiping her eyes. "It wasn't a joke, I swear," she said. "I was really and truly trying to turn you into that Zebra guy."

George sank back against the couch cushions, tugging on his zebra ears. "So, you can't get rid of them?"

"They'll go away on their own in a few minutes, tops," B said. "Just sit tight."

George fidgeted with the armrest. B leaned back in her beanbag chair, waiting. Would the ears shrink, or just *poof,* disappear?

Either way, it didn't matter.

Any minute now.

How about . . . now?

Why haven't they disappeared?

Uh-oh . . .

"Kids!" Mr. Fitzsimmons's voice sounded from upstairs. "Chinese food's here! Come get an egg roll before I eat 'em all!"

George jumped up and started pacing around the rec room. "What'm I gonna do? What'll my parents say? How in the heck do I hide zebra ears?"

B looked around the basement. "Got any more hats?"

"Ha-ha," George snapped. "Very funny. You're not the one with zebra ears. At least you could *try* a spell to get rid of them."

"You really want me putting another spell on you?"

George looked at his watch. "It's been five minutes. If the effect was temporary, wouldn't they have vanished by now?"

B swallowed. "Probably." Some of George's anxiety was beginning to rub off on her. What if the ears didn't go away? What if they were still there *tomorrow*? A few people were bound to notice — in particular, Mr. Bishop, their English teacher who was secretly her witching tutor. And if he found out that she'd let slip about her magic . . . who knew what the M.R.S. would do to her!

B rubbed her hands together. "Okay, you ready? I'll give it a try."

George sat down, twisting an action figure in his hands. Fortunately, Zeus's waist swiveled.

"R-E-V-E-R-S-E."

No change to the ears, but a plastic armored tank began rolling backward across the carpet.

"Ha-ha," George said, not really laughing.

B licked her lips. "U-N-D-O."

Nope. George's shoelaces untied, though.

"U-N-Z-E-B-R-A."

"Unzebra?" George said, tugging on his new ears. "That's not even a word! What happens when you spell words that aren't words?"

"Nothing, apparently," B said, frowning at George's head. Tufts of black and white hair jutted up through his curls, while his new ears twitched at every sound in the room, almost with a life of their own.

"Looks like you may be wearing a hat for a while," B said. "I'm sure the ears'll go away. If not, I'll think of something." *With any luck*, B added silently, *before the Magical Rhyming Society finds out.*

"B-but, B!" George stammered. "You can't leave me like this! *Do* something! You're the witch!"

"I told you transformations were risky," B said sadly.

"Kung pao chicken, going once!" Mr. F bellowed from up the stairs. "Going twice!"

George found a hat, pulled it down hard over all four of his ears, and held the door open for B. "You will figure it out, won't you?"

B patted his shoulder, trying to sound surer than she felt. "I promise."

The next morning B waited anxiously at the bus stop, watching for George to appear. Her sombrero, worn for Crazy Hat Day, flapped in the wind. Her nerves danced like Mexican jumping beans in the pit of her stomach. *Please, please, let the ears be gone!*

The bus came, and there was still no sign of George, so she boarded and sat down. The bus started to leave, then the driver hit the brakes and opened the door once more. A disheveled-looking George climbed on board.

"Hey, everybody, look at George," Jason Jameson yelled. "He thinks it's Christmas! Nice earmuffs, Fitzsimmons! You call that a hat? Gonna make a snowman out of leaves?"

George ducked into B's seat and slid down so his head didn't show. B leaned over the back of the seat to glare at Jason, then looked at George anxiously. He wore a blue knit ski cap over his head and a fuzzy red pair of earmuffs over his ears — his *human* ears.

B bit her lower lip. "Let me guess . . ."

George nodded miserably. "They're still there. Do you know how much you hear with two sets of ears? I could barely get to sleep last night. Every little creak in the house, every car passing by . . . it was horrible."

B sighed. "That explains the earmuffs."

"Yup. I figured all the noise on the bus would make me crazy. As it is, I can still hear Mona Blair in the backseat, telling Allie Rogers that" — he cocked his head to one side — "Trevor Harding is 'totally hot.' *Blech*." He shuddered. "Way more info than I needed."

B sank lower in her seat. She tried to think of a way to change the subject. "Got any chocolate?" she said.

He shook his head. "Nope. I'm in no mood for chocolate today."

B chewed on a knuckle and tried to think. The day her best friend, George, was in no mood for chocolate might as well be the day sunshine was abolished forever. It couldn't, and shouldn't, happen.

She racked her brain to think of spells that might fix the problem. Barely moving her lips, she thought about George's zebra ears and whispered faintly, "N-O-R-M-A-L. D-I-S-A-P-P-E-A-R. R-E-V-E-R-S-E." But those bumpy spots under his ski cap remained. Fortunately, she figured, no one else would be likely to realize something was unusual.

"I can hear you, you know," George muttered. "Nice try, but it's not working."

B slumped even lower. "Sorry, George. I'll figure something out."

Chapter 4

"Just because you're wearing goofy hats today doesn't excuse you from paying attention," Mr. Bishop said, tapping the wide brim of the Stetson hat he had on — black, matching his sweater and jeans, as well as his horn-rimmed rectangular glasses and glossy, pointed beard. "Am I the only person here who isn't obsessed with Thursday's game?"

"Pretty much," Jamal Burns said. The class giggled.

Mr. Bishop was right — with the buildup of Spirit Week leading to the championship game, everyone was having trouble thinking about science or math. Now it was English class, and B was distracted, too, but not by soccer. She had zebras on the brain.

"Observe," Mr. Bishop said, removing his Stetson hat and holding it up so the class could see the inside. B knew another one of Mr. Bishop's "magic" tricks was on the way — except she knew what kind of magic Mr. Bishop really could do.

"See anything inside this hat?" They all shook their heads. "Miss Springbranch, will you make sure? Check the lining, please."

Jenny Springbranch examined the hat and handed it back, shaking her head. "Nothing."

"You're quite sure?"

Jenny nodded.

Mr. Bishop frowned at the inside of the hat, shook it upside down, then scowled inside it once more. Muttering to himself, he reached inside and pulled out a soccer ball.

"No way," George whispered.

"How d'you *do* that?"

"It's impossible!"

Mr. Bishop tossed the ball to George, who caught it. He spun it around to show everyone the GO,

TIGERS inscribed on one panel in permanent marker.

"Thanks, Mr. Bishop!" George said. "Wow!"

The class applauded, and Mr. Bishop took a bow. Then he said, "Now that we've gotten soccer out of our heads, for the moment, I want you to follow me to the computer lab. We'll practice conducting research online. Next month's project is to write a research paper. You'll need to pick a subject to write about, research it, and write a three-page paper."

There were groans and protests as their class shuffled down the hall toward the computer lab, but B didn't mind the assignment. She knew exactly what she'd be researching.

Zebras.

There was a new bounce in B's step. Of course! She needed more facts about zebras. That was probably why she couldn't undo the curse yet — she was dealing with subjects she didn't fully understand.

Well, it might help anyway.

She and George found computers right next to each other and logged in. While Mr. Bishop was lecturing the class on how to choose trustworthy sources for facts online, she quickly went to her favorite online encyclopedia and softly typed "zebra" in the search field.

Oh, rats.

There were lots of kinds of zebras.

Well, let's see. She looked more closely. There were three species of zebra, and several subspecies. The different types had English names and Latin names. She scrolled up and down, scanning the pictures to see if any of the different types had ears just like George's.

That was the problem — they all did. B stuck her hand underneath her sombrero and scratched her head.

George peered over at her screen. "Find anything useful?"

B dreaded facing George. He still had on those silly earmuffs. She kept her eyes glued to the screen. "This is sad!" she whispered. "One subspecies of zebra, the quagga, has already gone extinct! And the Grevy's zebra is endangered."

George adjusted his glasses, which kept sliding down his nose. "They all look the same to me."

"Yeah, but they're different," B explained. "There are three main species of zebra: Plains, Mountain, and Grevy's. Subspecies, too . . . the, um, Dauw, Burchell's zebra, Chapman's zebra, Wahlberg's zebra, Selous's zebra, Grant's zebra . . ."

"Shhh," George hissed.

B looked up to see Mr. Bishop peering down at her from under his Stetson. "Oops," she said, feeling her cheeks grow hot.

Mr. Bishop grinned. "You're doing great research, B," he said, "but keep it down, okay? Especially when I'm still lecturing. Zebras, is it?"

B nodded. *Please, oh, please, let me figure out how to get rid of those ears before Mr. Bishop finds out what I've done. . . .*

For the rest of the class, B read everything she could find about zebras, copying the list of zebra names on a sheet of paper, in English and Latin. When the bell rang, everyone filed out of the computer room, but B tugged George's sleeve.

"Let me try this," she said. And, tacking a "U-N" before each name, she rattled through the list, thinking about George's ears. *Equus quagga*, Grevy's zebra, Hartmann's mountain zebra, she spelled them all.

"Well," George said, patting his ski cap, "the ears are still there."

B sighed. "That's probably because those aren't really words anyway." She snapped her fingers. "Let me try one other thing, okay? Take your hat off again."

George complied. Staring hard at George's ears, B spelled the word slowly and carefully. "D-I-S-A-P-P-E-A-R."

The ears vanished.

"Holy cats!" B whooped for joy. "Look at yourself, George! They're gone!" The worry B had been feeling all day about getting caught suddenly disappeared. She had gotten away with it.

George stared at the dim reflection of himself in the window. "Are they really gone? I can still hear like crazy. When you hollered, you just about busted my zebra eardrums." He inspected his face and profile more closely. "But they're gone, aren't they?"

"Not a trace of zebra ears," B said proudly. What a relief!

"Today's pizza day," George said. "Let's go before the mega-meat pie's all gone." He turned toward the door.

That's when B saw it.

"Eep!" B couldn't help herself. The sound slipped out.

"What's the matter?"

B stood and pointed toward her own lower back. George twisted and craned his neck to see . . . a zebra tail, poking out through a new hole in his jeans!

George stared at B.

B stared back, feeling her elation crash to dread. "Oops?" she said.

" 'Oops?' " George repeated. " 'Oops?' I've got a tail now. A *tail*! Make it go away, quick!"

B, still shell-shocked by this new development, shook her head feebly. "I don't think I dare try." Turning the ears into a tail was *not* good progress, and who knew what zebra feature would come next if she took the risk.

George twisted around and wiggled until he could stuff the tail down into his jeans.

Why can't I control my magic? B thought despairingly.

Finally George pulled off his "La Zebra" sweatshirt and tied it around his waist to hide the bumps and hole. "You are going to fix this, right, B? Because there's no hat I can put on over my backside, if you know what I mean."

B nodded. "I'll fix it, George," she said. "Somehow."

"Race you to the caf, then," George said, and B, relieved that he wasn't too angry at her, nodded. They grabbed their bags and headed out the door.

B could never really beat George in a race — he was the sixth-grade champion in the fifty-yard dash — but today George had nearly reached the end of the long hallway before B had even gotten halfway. He was flying!

Galloping, more like. Like a horse.

Like a zebra.

Chapter 5

After school, George took off to the athletic fields for soccer practice, and B headed to Mr. Bishop's room for magic tutoring. She always looked forward to her magical studies, and she'd never needed instruction more than today. But she almost dreaded today's session. It felt as though she had something to hide from him. Well, she did . . . George's tail! And that was the very reason she needed so much help.

But how could she ask Mr. Bishop for help without him figuring out what she'd done? She tried to picture the scenario: "Suppose, Mr. Bishop, I were to turn my best friend, who's nonmagical, into a zebra? How would I fix that problem?"

Nope. No good.

She would just have to figure it out on her own, as long as things didn't get any worse. If they did, B would *have* to confess, and face whatever consequences there were for breaking the no-telling rule.

She reached the classroom and sat down next to Mozart, the class's hamster, who lived in a cage on the windowsill. She and Mozart were old friends — in fact, the opinionated hamster had helped her solve her first magical mess. At the sight of B, the hamster stood on his hind legs and waved a paw, his tiny nose quivering.

She reached in and pulled him out, nestling him in the palm of her hand.

"S-P-E-A-K," she said after checking to make sure no one was lingering in the room.

"Hiya, Missy," Mozart said, sniffing. "What's the matter with you? You look like someone's fed you bad lettuce. Chin up! Want a kibble? Help yourself."

"No thanks, Mozart," she said. "I'm just worried. Know anything about fixing magical spells that've gone screwball?"

"Hey, I'm just a hamster. What do I know about

magic?" he said. "Food, that's what I know. You got to keep your strength up. Spend at least half your day eating, that's my advice, and the other half sleeping. You do that, you've got no problems."

B shook her head and rubbed her cheek against Mozart's soft fur. "That's not such a good idea for humans. We're supposed to do more than just eat and sleep."

"That's why you get yourselves into such trouble," Mozart sniffed. "But what do I know? I'm just a hamster."

"But for a hamster," Mr. Bishop said from the doorway, "you sure have a lot to say." He took off his Stetson and hung it from a peg by the door. He smiled at B. "Caught you off guard, didn't I? No worries. But be careful, B, to make sure nonmagical people don't accidentally discover what your spelling can do. "

B gulped. *If only you knew*, she thought.

"Sorry, Mozart," she whispered. "S-P-E-E-C-H-L-E-S-S," she spelled, and stroking the hamster between the ears with her pinky finger, she placed him gently back in the cedar chips at the bottom of his cage.

Mr. Bishop sat in a student desk opposite B. "Well, B, how's life?"

B shrugged. "It's okay."

He watched her closely. "Are you sure? You don't seem like yourself today. Is something on your mind?"

Oh, man, was it that obvious? She already felt guilty enough without his psychic X-ray vision peering into her brain and figuring out the truth.

"I'm looking forward to reading your zebra research paper," Mr. Bishop added.

At the word "zebra," B flinched. She rapidly changed the subject. "I've got a, uh, question I've been meaning to ask you."

"Shoot."

B twisted her fingers underneath her desk. "It seems like I do all these spells, and they don't usually come out quite right." Good, good. A safe approach so far.

Mr. Bishop smiled. "That's typical for beginner

witches. I seem to recall *someone* spelling the word 'chaos' and setting off the school's fire alarm. . . ." His dark eyes sparkled.

B smiled, remembering when she didn't know she had her magic and had caused all sorts of trouble. "Exactly. How do you, er, clean up a magical mess? Reverse a bad spell? Things like that?"

Mr. Bishop cracked his knuckles. "Good question. In the case of the fire alarm, we just rode it out, didn't we? Waited for the alarm to stop, and for all the water to get mopped up."

B swallowed hard. "But what if it doesn't go away on its own?"

"Most spells can be undone," Mr. Bishop said, "but sometimes a witch gets in over her head and the Magical Rhyming Society Dismantle Squad has to be called in."

B's mouth went dry. "Dismantle Squad?"

Mr. Bishop laughed. "Don't let the name scare you. Usually, they are only there to help."

B tried to smile, but the "usually" worried her. If she had to face the Dismantle Squad, *what* exactly would they be dismantling? Her . . . or George? She didn't want to think about either.

Something else was bothering B. "What did you mean by 'most' spells? Any spell *can* be undone, can't it?"

Mr. Bishop twirled the tip of his beard. "There have been some famous cases of irreversible spells, usually when witches attempt magic too advanced for them," he said. "There's a fascinating book about it at the M.R.S. library — often the spells start to intensify the more the witch tries to reverse them."

Irreversible spells. Witches attempting advanced magic . . .

"Don't worry, B," Mr. Bishop said. "The kind of spells I'm teaching you aren't likely to do permanent damage." He rose. "Now, let's get started on today's lesson. First, we're going to try something a little exciting. . . . Most witches your age can't do this, but you just might." He paused, and B smiled weakly. "I want to see what happens if you attempt a traveling spell. So we're going to see if you can magically transport us to the Magical Rhyming Society without my help. Once we get there, we'll pay a visit to the library and learn how to conduct magical research."

B had to put irreversible spells, the Dismantle Squad, and George's zebra tail out of her head. She had to focus if she wasn't going to let Mr. Bishop see how nervous she was.

"Okay." B placed her sombrero on her desk and stood up. "What do I do?"

"Well, that's the question," Mr. Bishop said. "For other students, I encourage them to compose a rhyming couplet that will take them there. For you, we'll need to find the right combination of thoughts and a word to spell. I would imagine you'd think hard about the M.R.S., then spell 'travel.' How does that sound?"

"It sounds awfully simple," B said.

"Often, the simplest spells are the most effective," her teacher said. "Hold on to my sleeve so you take me with you, and give it a whirl."

B clutched the sleeve of Mr. Bishop's sweater, closed her eyes, and tried to think about the Magical Rhyming Society. Her mind was jumpy with worries about zebra George, but she focused on the M.R.S. It was a happy place to think about. No other place B knew was so, well, magical! All those rhyming witches experimenting with magical methods everywhere you turned . . . something interesting was always happening.

"Are you worried?" Mr. Bishop asked.

B opened her eyes, hesitated, then shook her head.

"Don't worry, B," her teacher said. "Relax, and trust yourself! You've got powers most young witches take years to develop. Believe me. Believe in *yourself.*"

"Okay," B said, scrunching her eyes shut once more. *M.R.S.!* she thought.

"T-R-A-V-E-L," she spelled.

She felt the magical travel cyclone whip around them both, plastering her dark hair across her face.

But the wind didn't die down when it normally would have.

Cautiously, B opened her eyes.

Uh-oh.

Chapter 6

They'd traveled to the school athletic fields, landing right behind the bleachers, only yards away from where George's soccer team was practicing. B dropped Mr. Bishop's sleeve like a hot potato.

Her teacher was turning every which way, peering with hawk's eyes at everyone in sight. B knew what he was doing. He was checking to see if anyone on the soccer field had noticed them appear out of thin air. B followed his lead, but no one seemed to be watching, or indeed taking any notice of them at all.

"Looks like we're clear," Mr. Bishop said. "Whew! That was a little close for comfort!"

"Figures I'd mess this up," B muttered to herself. She kicked at a tuft of crabgrass.

Mr. Bishop turned toward her, surprised. "Why would you say that, B?"

B blushed. She hadn't realized her teacher could hear her. "I . . . just . . . when I use magic, I always seem to cause trouble."

Mr. Bishop placed a hand on her shoulder. "That's not true," he said. "B, your magic is extraordinary. Every beginner witch starts out with some mishaps. Part of learning to master your magic is just learning to trust yourself. Learning to relax and focus. You can do it, B." He scanned the surroundings one more time. "I think we're clear. No one seems to have seen us."

"If someone had seen us, couldn't you just . . . magically alter their memories or something?" B asked.

Mr. Bishop shook his head firmly. "No, and please don't ever attempt such a thing, B," he said. "To use magic to alter a human in some way — either in mind, or in body — that's extremely risky.

Only the most advanced witches, with years of training, and *with a compelling reason*, should ever even *think* about it."

"Oh," B said, her mind reeling. "Right."

Her teacher stopped scanning the horizon. "Think of the Three High Dictums of magic that you learned from Madame Mellifluous," he said. "Can you tell me what they are?"

B nodded. "You can't make something out of nothing. Don't use magic to harm others. And don't let nonmagical people find out about magic." She didn't dare look at Mr. Bishop, lest he see the guilt written in her eyes. She'd broken two of the Three High Dictums with her spell on George. Her jangling stomach felt like an erupting volcano.

"Right. Just think of the harm that erasing people's memories could cause. That would definitely be a case for the Dismantle Squad."

B tried not to panic. She was just going to have to reverse her spell before anyone found out about it and alerted the Dismantle Squad.

"Let's head back inside," Mr. Bishop said, "using our feet, not spells." He set off toward the school.

"I'll take us to the M.R.S., and then I want to give you a tour of the library. I can show you how to do research and then you can look into all this reversing spells stuff that you're wondering about."

B felt a hint of relief. If there was anywhere she'd find the solution to her problem, it would be in the M.R.S. library. Everything would be okay as long as Mr. Bishop didn't figure out why she wanted to know so badly.

As she followed her teacher, she turned back and caught sight of George, galloping down the field, dribbling a soccer ball. The scrimmaging team members chased after him but he was yards ahead of them. He sprinted like a wild animal.

What had she done?

Mr. Bishop followed her gaze out to the soccer field. "Your friend George is quite the speed demon, isn't he?"

B swallowed. "Um, yeah." They entered the building and set off down the hall toward Mr. Bishop's room. Was he suspicious of George's speed? She forced out a laugh. "That George! Been winning races ever since he could walk."

Mr. Bishop gazed at her thoughtfully. "Is that so?"

B's insides squirmed. Was her teacher just being a good listener, or could he see right through her?

They reached the classroom.

"Grab my sleeve, B," Mr. Bishop said. "Here we go.

"The M.R.S. library's our destination.
Research is vital to B's education!"

Once again the wind arose. This time it deposited them in the great circular library that was the centerpiece of the entire Magical Rhyming Society.

"Here we are," Mr. Bishop said.

"Doug? Doug Bishop. It's really you!" A burly man in camouflage robes and a flattop haircut appeared. He seized Mr. Bishop's hand, shaking it heartily and slapping him on the shoulder. Mr. Bishop nearly buckled under the impact.

"Dirk," B's teacher managed to gasp. "Good to see you, Dirk! How long has it been?"

"Not since fencing team, back in college!"

The two men were soon lost in conversation about old friends, and B's attention started to drift to the shelves and shelves of books that surrounded her. She knew the answer to all her troubles had to be right here, in this magnificent library. While her teacher was dodging Dirk's reenactments of their fencing duels, she approached the nearest set of shelves.

To her surprise, a short stepladder slid over toward her and nudged her ankles like a friendly little terrier. She stepped on it, and it began to grow taller as it wheeled her around the circumference of the great library tower. "Hey, thanks!" she told it, just in case it could hear. In a place like this library, you couldn't be sure.

She spiraled slowly up the stacks, scanning the ornate books. They were nothing like the books in a regular library or bookstore. Each book here was made by hand, with hand-carved details in the leather bindings and gemstone talismans embedded in the spines.

Her roving ladder seemed to know instinctively when B wanted to read a title more carefully, and it paused before moving on. What would she give for time to read all of these books! Especially *Revenge with Rutabagas and Other Produce Concoctions Your Tutor Never Taught You.*

B giggled. She'd have to remember that one for later.

Halfway up the tower, when B was starting to feel a touch of vertigo from the dizzying height, her ladder stopped in front of a dragon-scale green–covered book called *Undoing Magic Spells.*

This is it! B felt a wave of relief. Here at her fingertips was the information she needed to turn George back into himself.

"How did you know what I needed?" B whispered to the ladder, but it didn't answer.

She reached for the book, but a shimmery film suddenly appeared, blocking her fingers. It was soft to the touch, and it looked no thicker than spiderwebs, but it would neither yield nor let B grab the volume.

B pulled her hand away, and the film vanished.

She reached up again, and the magical barrier zapped her!

"Ow!"

"*Ahem.*" B looked down to see an older witch in maroon robes whose ladder was swiveling past just underneath B's. Her lips were pinched tightly together, her face disapproving. B lowered her hand and looked around the room in what she hoped was an innocent way until the maroon witch's ladder passed.

Only then did she realize that the people on ladders weren't removing books from the shelves. They were only browsing. When they got off the ladders, they lined up in front of the circulation desk, where they waited for a turn to browse the hundreds of tiny card catalog drawers. B stepped down for a closer view, and noticed her ladder shrinking as she did so.

"Thanks again," she told it when it was little more than a footstool. She could have sworn it nodded, in a laddery sort of way.

Chapter 7

B stood, watching the other witches in the library, wondering how she was going to get to that book, when Mr. Bishop appeared at her side.

"Hi, Mr. Bishop," B said. "Did you have fun with Dirk?"

"Hah," her teacher said, rubbing his arm. "I'm lucky I survived. How'd you make out?"

"I've had a good look, but why can't I take books off the shelves?"

Mr. Bishop smiled. "It used to be that you could take any book off the shelves," he explained, "but just like other libraries, there were problems with books not coming back on time, books getting lost, et cetera. Then, the librarians put overdue curses on the books, giving borrowers purple pimples or itchy rashes, but the nineteen twenty-nine Council on Witch Rights decided that was unethical. So, now we do things differently."

"Meaning, you don't let the books off the shelves?"

Mr. Bishop laughed. "No, no. Look around you!" He pointed toward dozens of witches, seated at tables and reading. "The way we do it is . . ." He snapped his fingers. "Better yet, I'll let you figure it out. You're a word fan. You'll love this."

They approached the card catalog and stood where they could watch. B saw each witch approach the shelves in turn, pull open an alphabetized drawer, and speak some words — perhaps the title of a book?

B peered around the arm of a tall witch dressed in yellow to watch more closely. Out from the card catalog drawer poured a silky gray vapor that formed into a cloud. Inside the cloud, a hazy face appeared, its hair pulled back into a tight bun, with bifocals on a string perched on the end of its nose.

"Your selection, please?" the face said.

The witch who had summoned the librarian's head spoke. "Fleeciest Sulphur Show Too."

Huh? B glanced up at Mr. Bishop, but he only grinned at her. He wasn't giving her any clues.

The librarian's face nodded, and the witch making the request stepped to the end of a table while the head in the cloud zoomed through the air, reaching nearly to the topmost stacks.

Fleeciest Sulphur Show Too? B thought. It could be the name of a witching book, but what on earth could it teach? Sulphur — alchemy, perhaps? But *fleeciest?* How weird!

On a counter that ran alongside the line of waiting witches, B saw pencil stubs and slips of paper scattered about, with letters scribbled and apparently reordered. Odd. Maybe the library patron witches got tired of waiting so they played word games to amuse themselves.

The cloud floated back and dropped a book into the witch's waiting hands. B was just able to glimpse the cover. The book was called: *Eel Soup for the Witch's Soul.*

B was baffled.

Mr. Bishop struggled not to laugh.

The next witch advanced to the card catalog; he was about B's age and looked like he knew exactly what he was doing. He opened a different drawer, and a cloud appeared with a different face inside. Instead of bifocals, this one wore a monocle and mustache. A much older librarian, B decided.

"Soup in Flowerpot, please," the witch said.

The librarian removed his monocle and frowned. "We have no such volume in our collection."

The witch frowned and then realization came over his face. "I'm sorry. Scratch the 'please.' Just: 'Soup in Flowerpot.'"

"Ah." The cloud whizzed off to another corner and returned carrying *Powerful Potions*. B was starting to get an idea. She saw witches casually working out their word puzzles on slips of paper, as if they hadn't a care in the world. B thought about the book titles: *Soup in Flowerpot* brought down *Powerful Potions*. P, O, W, E, R . . . B started to see the letters individually.

B grabbed a slip of paper and wrote both sets of words, one above the other. Her pencil flew as she crossed out one letter at a time in each row. First the S. Then the O and U. Yep. They were all there.

"That's right," Mr. Bishop said. "You're getting it now."

"It's an anagram!" B declared.

"Shh," Mr. Bishop said as heads all around them turned to stare.

"It's an anagram," B repeated in a careful whisper. "A letter scramble."

"Bingo!" Mr. Bishop replied. "I knew you'd figure it out." He consulted his watch. "It's time for us to be heading back. Seeing my old friend Dirk didn't help today's session, but I'm glad you got to have a look around the library."

B didn't want to go so quickly. She wanted to check out that *Undoing Magic Spells* book, but she couldn't let on to Mr. Bishop how important it was and decided she would just have to get back as soon as she could.

She followed her teacher over to an area where their traveling spell wouldn't ruffle anyone's papers.

"Mr. Bishop," B said before he began his couplet,

"why on earth would they make you do anagrams to take books out?"

"It was the dying wish of a quirky head librarian, almost a century ago," Mr. Bishop said. "He thought book borrowers needed more incentive to appreciate the resources provided, so he wanted to make people work for the books they needed — and a way to keep the librarians' brains active. After all, they have to solve each anagram correctly!"

Chapter 8

"Morning!" George cried, sailing past B at the bus stop. He skidded to a halt, then swiveled and pranced back to where B stood. It was Costume Day for Spirit Week and B was dressed as a Halloween witch. George, B realized with a shock, wore a pair of red devil's horns on his head, and his tail was poking out through a hole in his pants for all the school to see!

"What are you doing?" she hissed as the bus rounded the corner. "I can see your tail!"

"So can the world," George said, smiling. "I'm a devil! Isn't it great?"

B frowned. "Sort of," she said, "except that your tail twitches."

George waved this obstacle away. "Not much. I could say it's battery-powered. I used charcoal dust to smudge it all dark, so no one would see the stripes. I tried to make it red, but the stripes still showed through."

"But, George," B said, lowering her voice to a whisper, "if Mr. Bishop figures out what I've done . . . I'll get in enormous trouble!" She swallowed hard, thinking of the Dismantle Squad.

They boarded the bus, and George had to sit awkwardly to avoid squashing his tail. "It'll be okay," he said. "I figured it was better to let the tail show and say it's for Costume Day, than to keep trying to hide it." He grinned. "Besides, I'm starting not to mind it so much. The ears are gone but I can still hear as though they're there, and it comes in handy sometimes. And the speed? I'm faster than I've ever been. I've got more kicking power, more endurance . . . it's like I'm really turning into La Zebra!"

"Shh!" B hissed, looking around to see if anyone heard.

George laughed. It came out like a braying bark. His eyes grew wide, then he laughed some more.

"You're not turning into *La Zebra Italiana*," B whispered. "You're turning into a zebra, as in, a stripy horsey thing that lives on the plains of Africa."

"It won't last forever, though," George said. "You said so yourself."

"Right," B said, shrinking down in the bus seat. She couldn't bring herself to tell George what she'd learned about irreversible spells. Did going from zebra ears to a zebra tail count as "intensifying" like Mr. Bishop had said? B hoped not.

The bus arrived at the school, and George sauntered off down the aisle, leaving B musing. There was still the Magical Rhyming Society to deal with if anyone ever found out what she'd done. B started to think that she might be in over her head, but then she remembered the book in the library. All she had to do was get that book, and everything would be okay. But she wouldn't be able to go back until at least after school. Would George's tail be able to make it through a whole day at school, without giving everything away?

She scurried off the bus and ran to catch up with George. She found him at his locker, chewing noisily on a lettuce leaf.

B stopped in her tracks. "George, *what* are you eating?" she demanded. "Where's your stash of Enchanted Chocolates?"

George shrugged and stuffed another lettuce leaf in his mouth. "Don't feel much like chocolate these days," he said. "Candy's bad for athletes."

B put her hand on George's forehead. "Now I know you're seriously sick."

"Nah, I'm not. But my mom had this great romaine in the crisper. Want some?"

B shook her head. "No thanks. I like my lettuce with ranch dressing and croutons. Not for a morning snack."

"Suit yourself," George said. "More for me."

The bell rang. "You'd better hurry," B said. "Why don't you save some lettuce for Mozart?"

George shrugged. "Okay. See you in English."

B thought about George's dilemma at every spare moment in homeroom. And all through English class she waited for Mr. Bishop to comment on George's zebra tail, but he showed no sign of suspecting it was anything other than a part of George's costume. When the bell rang and everyone had left the room, B held George back.

She had to end this chaos once and for all, and she had an idea of how she might do it, even without the book. Mr. Bishop had said that the simplest spells are the most effective. A bag-cauldron concoction got her into this mess — wouldn't another bag-cauldron concoction be the simplest way out?

While B thought, George pulled a large zippered baggie out of his backpack and began to munch. A scrabbling noise came from the back of the classroom. Mozart had seen the lettuce and was clawing at the glass wall of his cage.

"Okay, little fella," George said. "I'll share." George took Mozart out and held him while feeding him small pieces of romaine.

"I've had an idea for a way to turn you back into a one hundred percent human," B said. "It won't take more than a minute."

"Hope it doesn't work," George said, watching Mozart closely. "Coach said yesterday was my best practice in weeks."

B wasn't interested in debating him. The Dismantle Squad wouldn't stand around talking, and Mr. Bishop certainly wouldn't, either, if he found out that she'd revealed her magic to a nonwitch.

B dumped the contents of her and George's backpacks onto her desk, looking for things to use in her bag-cauldron. From the pile of rubble she picked a half-empty pouch of Enchanted Chocolate Smooches and a stick-figure doodle George had drawn of himself kicking a goal, and put them all into her backpack. It felt like her spell needed one more thing, for good luck.

A coppery glint on the floor supplied an idea. A penny! Finding one was lucky, wasn't it? She spun it into the air with a flick of her thumb, just for fun. Oops! It landed in Mozart's cage.

She fished it out from the cedar chips, wiped off the flecks of dust and hair that clung to it, and tossed it into her backpack-cauldron.

Ready.

She watched George pet Mozart's soft orange fur, and filled her mind with the image of her best friend, looking like his normal self.

"H-U-M-A-N," she spelled.

His tail didn't vanish. But it twitched in astonishment.

Sitting on George's lap, where the hamster had been, was a kid in an orange tracksuit with a white collar, and a leaf of lettuce dangling from his mouth!

B blinked.

"M-Mozart?"

Chapter 9

"Holy cats!" B cried.

The kid in the tracksuit sniffed the air, revealing protruding buckteeth. George stood up suddenly, and the kid, still chewing his greens, stumbled to his feet. He turned and grabbed at George's bag of lettuce.

"Gimme some more of that lettuce action! I don't know when I've ever been so hungry."

George, in a daze, still held the bag back, away from Mozart — or rather, the kid Mozart had become.

"Oh, come on. What's the matter? Is that the last bunch of lettuce on earth or something? Bet you got a whole backyard full of it at home." Mozart's nose twitched. He turned and waved at B. "Hiya, Missy, did you turn yourself small all of a sudden? You gotta watch out with those spells of yours." He clutched his stomach and bent over, laughing. "You turned this guy" — he pointed a thumb at George — "into a horse, ain't ya? One of them stripy horses you see in pictures? I smelled him yesterday when he came into class. Mr. Big Teacher Man, he's so smart, even he doesn't notice there's a stripy horse in his class!"

And please, keep it that way, B thought, wringing her hands. *But what am I going to do about* you? *This is terrible! What if Mr. Bishop comes back in the room?*

Mozart caught sight of George stuffing his lettuce back into his backpack, and pounced on the pack before George could zip it shut. "You got anything else in there? Carrots? Peppers? C'mon, bub, I'm starving!"

George gave up and handed Mozart the lettuce bag, giving B a helpless look.

"Mmph," Mozart said, chewing and spraying

little bits of lettuce. "That's good stuff. One time someone brought me some *zoo . . . zoo . . .* zucchini, that's it. *That's* something a hamster doesn't taste every day."

Just then, Mozart noticed his hands. He held them up before his face in wonder.

"I ain't a hamster anymore, am I?" he breathed. "I'm a . . . one of *you*." He gazed down at his feet, and the tall orange-clad body in between. He poked at his own ribs and shoulders. "This real?" he asked.

B gulped. "Apparently."

Mozart spun around, spreading his arms wide, letting out a yell. "Whooooooopeeeee!"

George and B looked at each other in alarm. George bolted for the classroom door and shut it, peering through the window to see if any teachers had heard Mozart holler.

Mozart sprang toward the chalkboard and grabbed a new piece of chalk. "I *always* wanted to do this," he said, and snapped the chalk in half. He dropped one half on the floor and stomped it to powder, all the while laughing shrilly. Taking the other stumpy piece of chalk, he drew huge looping scribbles all over the board. "I'm gonna learn how to write for real, and then I'm gonna leave everyone notes telling 'em what I really think about 'em." He scowled. "Especially that bratty boy who's always poking pencils at me."

"Jason," George and B said in unison.

Mozart ran to Mr. Bishop's desk, bouncing and swiveling in the big office chair. He opened drawers and riffled through the papers, spilling some to the floor, and then stood on the seat of Mr. Bishop's chair, jumping high while the springs squeaked, still laughing that maniac laugh.

George and B raced to the desk to try to clean up the mess. George elbowed B. *"Do something!"*

"Right," B said, her mouth dry as the cedar chips in Mozart's cage. "I'll . . . do something." *We all know how well that'll work*, she thought. She cleared her throat and fixed her gaze on Mozart. "H-A-M- . . ."

Mozart stopped jumping and pointed an accusing finger at her. "No, you don't," he shouted. "I ain't going back in that cage again! I'm FREE, and no witch-girl or stripy-horse-boy is gonna stop me!" And, taking a flying leap off Mr. Bishop's seat, he raced toward the door, wrenched it open, and took off running down the hall.

Chapter 10

Mozart was gone.

Because of B's spelling, a ham sandwich appeared on Mr. Bishop's desk. Without thinking, George snagged the sprig of parsley on the plate and ate it.

"Now what?" George said.

"Catch him!" B cried.

"You want me to tackle him in the middle of the long hallway?"

"Pretty much," B said. "Just don't get caught, and don't hurt him. But you've got to get him back here, where I can transform him back into a hamster."

George shouldered his backpack. "What if you can't? What if he's stuck a human, just like I'm stuck a zebra?"

B closed her eyes. "Don't say things like that, George," she said. "We've got to stay positive. I'll change him back, and I'll change you back, too. I swear. But for now, use that supernatural speed of yours and *find that hamster* before he tells the whole school that I'm a witch and you're a zebra!"

George nodded. "The teachers are bound to notice the strange new kid in orange," he said. "If he keeps up this loony stuff, he'll get triple detention in the next five minutes." He went to the door. "Catch up to me, okay?"

B nodded and hurried to tidy up Mr. Bishop's desk, while George galloped after the human hamster in a tracksuit. *If I ever get out of this mess*, B vowed, *I will be a good little witch who practices her spelling lessons only at the M.R.S. and never takes risks like this again. I knew it was dangerous to try to make George a better soccer player. And see where it's led!*

Satisfied that the room was tidy enough, B grabbed her things and took off after George and Mozart. She wished she had George's supersonic hearing, because there was no sight of either boy.

Fortunately, the halls were empty, with most of the sixth-graders already at lunch. B ran as quickly and softly as she could through the school, glancing down each side hallway.

She was just passing the music wing when she heard a braying sound. Sure enough, at the end of the hall was a tall form with devil's horns and a moving tail. She turned on her heel and scooted down the hall toward her best friend.

George saw her coming and waited for her. "He just ran into the band room," he panted. "He's trapped in there."

"Well, here goes," B said. "Let's see if our Mozart is a music lover like his namesake."

They tiptoed in the room. There was no sign of Mozart. The empty band room looked strange with all the instruments abandoned, the chairs and music stands standing in crooked rows, a few sheets of handwritten musical scores scattered on the floor. George peeked under the bell of a giant tuba, and B grinned.

"A kid couldn't fit under a tuba, silly," she whispered.

"What if he's a hamster again?"

"Then this is our lucky day."

They checked under the xylophone and the marimba. No Mozart. They peered behind the piano, and in back of the sheet music shelves.

"Are you sure he came in here?" B asked.

"Positive!" George rubbed his head, where the zebra ears used to be. "Shh . . . I hear something."

B didn't hear anything.

"This way," George said, and headed for the corner where the percussion instruments were stashed.

Then B heard it, too. A little *ker-thump*, followed by a metallic *chingaring*.

"He just bumped into the cymbals," George whispered. Then, without warning, he lunged for the big bass drum, swiveling it around to reveal a folded-up kid in an orange tracksuit.

"Sur-PRISE! Hee hee hee!" Mozart sprang up like a jack-in-the-box and raced, giggling, past George and B, toward the door.

"H-A-M-S-T . . ." B cried, but he was already gone.

George and B looked at each other for a stunned second, then bolted after him. They only just saw him turn the corner, so they knew which direction he was headed.

"No!" B cried. "Not the cafeteria!"

They rounded the corner just in time to see the double doors bang shut behind Mozart. George sprinted ahead. By the time B got there, Mozart was nowhere to be seen. The cafeteria was full of its usual mayhem — worse today, perhaps, than normal. It must have been the costumes. Everyone seemed noisier and sillier than usual.

Nuggets and fries were on today's menu and B didn't have to read the menu board to know it. From the looks of the floor, several minor food fights had just recently finished, and chunks of fried food were everywhere.

George walked up and down the rows of tables, looking and listening for Mozart. Other boys — soccer players, most of them — struck up a "Go, Tigers" cheer at the sight of the popular team captain roving through the caf.

"Oh, for crying out loud." B ducked into the serving area and scanned the lunch line. No Mozart.

Meanwhile, the rest of the sixth grade had joined the cheering mob, their cries echoing off the walls. The cafeteria sounded like a World Cup soccer stadium.

"Qui-et!" Mrs. Gillet, the head lunch server, appeared in the doorway, waving a wooden spoon.

B met up with George by the side windows.

"I haven't seen him anywhere," George said. "You would think he'd be easy to spot in that neon orange suit. I don't get it! And with my, um, superhearing, this place is giving me a mega-headache."

"I'm sorry," B said. "But so long as you've already got the headache, try and see if you can hear anything that sounds like Mozart, will you?"

George closed his eyes and concentrated. B looked around anxiously to see if anyone had noticed that George's tail was behaving strangely.

George threw up his hands. "It's hopeless in here," he said.

B rubbed her temples. *Where would I go if I was a hamster-turned-kid? How would I feel in this crazy, noisy cafeteria if I had a rodent's brain?*

Scared, B decided. *So what would I do? Try to hide.*

B pretended to tie her shoes, and while she was crouching low, she scanned the jungle of sneakers and backpacks.

"Found him," she said, rising to her feet. "Let's go."

Chapter 11

B pulled George toward the far back corner of the cafeteria and sat down at the last seat, directing George to sit in the seat opposite her.

"Where is he?" he asked, perplexed.

"Right by your feet," B whispered.

Casually, as though she did this kind of thing normally, B poked her head under the table. Mozart was crouching, his arms wrapped around his ankles, his eyes wide with terror. Little whimpering sounds of fright came from his throat.

"Oh, Mozart!" B whispered. "What happened? Did someone hurt you?"

Mozart nodded. His eyes were rimmed with red. "All the noise hurts my ears!"

"Psst, B!"

B sat up straight. George was making strange faces at her, jerking his head toward the kids at the other end of their table, who were looking at B strangely.

"I know it looks weird," B whispered, "but we can't just leave him there! The poor thing's scared to death!"

"The poor thing," George replied, "is a tall sixth-grader who's crying under the table. How are you going to explain that?"

"Tell them he's your cousin," B said, "if you need to tell anyone anything. Find me a carrot, will you?"

George trotted to the salad bar while B tried to comfort Mozart, who was curled in a ball, chewing on his lower lip. *He's got the tracksuit on*, B thought, *but he's still more hamster than kid.* She held out her hand.

"Come on, Mozart," she crooned in a soft, soothing voice. "It's all right. You can come out now."

Mozart leaned toward her hand, almost sniffing it, his eyes wary and distrustful.

"I won't hurt you," B said. "I'm your friend, remember?"

Mozart hesitated.

George returned with two carrots, one that he ate himself, and another that he offered Mozart. The carrot tipped the scale. Mozart crawled out, clumsy and trembling, and snatched the carrot from B's hand. Then he let himself be guided to stand up and take a seat next to B. He hunkered down, gripping his carrot with both hands and stuffing it into his rapidly chewing mouth.

"Hey, what's with that kid?" a curly-haired boy from the end of the table asked. "His clothes are the same color as his favorite food, carrots!"

Mozart's head flew up. "Carrots? More carrots? Where?" He rose from his seat, sniffing the air, his nose twitching a mile a minute.

"The carrots are there, on the salad bar," the curly-haired boy said, pointing.

Mozart followed the kid's pointed finger, and gasped. His eyes bulged. His tongue hung out. "S-salad bar?"

B looked at George. "Oh, no!"

Mozart was already waddling off toward the salad bar, his arms outstretched like a zombie.

"Grab him, George!"

But before George could get far, the bell rang. Mozart never made it to the salad bar. He was swept out of the cafeteria on a surging tide of sixth-graders heading for their next class.

"What do we do?" George asked.

"You go ahead to gym," B said. "I'll search for Mozart. If I don't show up in a few minutes, though, get a hall pass and come looking for me, okay?"

George nodded and galloped off. B felt pretty sure that the zebra in George would hate missing gym even more than he'd hated to miss lunch.

B pressed her way through the hallways, scanning for a bright orange suit at every turn. Only when the halls had thinned out, after the bell rang, did B spot him, cringing, tucked into the recess in the wall next to a drinking fountain. Every time a nearby locker banged shut, Mozart jumped in fright.

"Poor Mozart," B said, approaching him slowly

so he wouldn't bolt away again. "You've had a rough day, haven't you?"

Mozart rubbed his eyes with the sides of his wrists, looking for all the world like his hamster self. "I wanna go back," he whimpered. "This place is wham-bang scary! People screaming like hawks about to attack, then they show you 'salad bars' and don't let you eat the lettuce." He sniffled. "I don't like it out here anymore."

B put her arm around Mozart's shoulder, not caring if anyone saw her, and steered him down the hall toward Mr. Bishop's room. *Please, oh, please let him not be there, or anyone else,* she thought. *And please, let my transforming spell work this time!*

And luck was with her. Once inside the room, she asked Mozart to sit on the window ledge next to his cage. "H-A-M-S-T-E-R," she spelled.

Mozart's head sunk into his shoulders, his feet gathered in toward his body, and in a blink, his orange suit disappeared and became his tawny coat of fur.

B scooped him up in both hands and nuzzled him against her cheek. "That's how I like you best," she said.

"Me, too," Mozart agreed.

"Oops!" B giggled. "I guess some changes like to stick around, don't they? S-P-E-E-C-H-L-E-S-S." She gently placed the silent hamster in his cage. He burrowed into a pile of shavings and vanished from sight.

Whew! B thought as she headed down the hall, late for gym. *But why, why was it so easy to transform Mozart back to himself, when I can't seem to fix George?*

Chapter 12

When B got home that afternoon, there was a fresh batch of pumpkin gingersnaps cooling on the counter, and a note that read, "Had to dash to the store. Need butter for buttercream frosting. Back in a few minutes. B, two cookies and that's IT! Love and kisses, Mom."

The first gingersnap was already disappearing down B's throat by the time she'd finished reading the note. She smiled, took off her witch costume, and poured herself a glass of milk. Pumpkin gingersnaps were just what B needed after a rough day like this one.

B poured the last bit of milk into her cup and set the empty jug in the crate to return it later. The store her mom had gone to, a specialty dairy shop that supplied all their milk, cream, butter, and cheese, was called the Magical Moo, and though they sold their products to nonwitches, the farmers that ran the dairy were a witching family just like B's. Her mom and Mrs. Colby were longtime friends from Witchin' Kitchen competitions, so B knew they would probably end up chatting away half the afternoon, maybe even sampling recipes.

What to do next? If only she'd been able to get a look inside that book, *Undoing Magic Spells.* And if only she could travel to the library and make an anagram to request it! But her traveling spells were as unpredictable as everything else she did magically. So no luck there.

B downed the milk, brushed cookie crumbs off her fingers, and headed up the stairs.

Just as she passed by Dawn's bedroom door, it flew open, and Dawn nearly plowed into B, just stopping in the nick of time.

"Geez, you startled me!" Dawn said.

"Sorry," B said. "Where are you in such a hurry to get to?"

"I'm heading off to the Magical Rhyming Society to do some group research on jinxes for a lab exam next week," Dawn said.

Perfect! "Can I come?" B asked. "Please?"

Dawn looked surprised. "Why would you want to?"

"I just want to . . . do some research of my own."

Dawn thought for a minute, then shrugged. "Sure, why not?"

They went back downstairs, and Dawn grabbed her purse while B jotted a scribble on the same notepaper their mother had left for them next to the cookies.

"Ready," she told Dawn.

"Hold my arm," Dawn said. "Here goes:

"We're off to a library where magical studies
Await us, along with our magical buddies."

The cyclone sped them off in a blink to the foyer of the great round library room at the Magical Rhyming Society, where bookshelves stretched up for what seemed like miles, and witches in sparkling robes scampered along rolling ladders to find rare and ancient volumes of spells. Behind them, a corridor led to classrooms and private study areas. Dawn's study session must be back that way.

B jabbed Dawn with a friendly elbow poke. *"Buddies?"*

"Well, it rhymes, anyway," Dawn said. "I've got friends here. Haven't you met any of the other witches your age yet? Are all your lessons still one-on-one?"

"I guess there aren't any other spelling witches my age," B said. "Or any age, for that matter."

"That's my sister," Dawn said, patting B proudly on the shoulder. "One of a kind. Listen, I've got to get with my group. You know what to do here, right?"

"Right."

"Okay. I'll probably be an hour."

B hurried to the table near the card catalog line, grabbed a paper and pencil, and got to work. She wrote UNDOING MAGIC SPELLS on her paper and stared at it for a while.

UNDOING MAGIC SPELLS

Hmm.

UNDOING MAGIC SPELLS

She crossed out the letters she'd already used. "G" plus "A" and "L" made "gal." Gal sings.

UNDOING MAGIC SPELLS

GAL SINGS

After a few false starts, B hit the jackpot with "melodic" and found that the letters remaining spelled "pun."

UNDOING MAGIC SPELLS

MELODIC GAL SINGS PUN

She grinned. It was only letters. B was a natural speller. She'd be an ace at this before long!

The line moved slowly, so B passed the time by trying another anagram with the same book title. There was definitely a knack to this that she could develop with more practice, she thought. She found "scolding," and, feeling very smug, realized she could make another -ing word out of "using." And the letters that remained spelled . . . "pleam"? "Lamep"? "Maple"!

Better yet, "Ample"!

And then it was her turn to face the librarian. Which drawer should she open? She hesitated, feeling nervous. Would she get another zap here if she did it wrong?

"Choose the drawer that matches the first letter of the title of your book," said a witch in yellow, just leaving with his title, *Magical Chromatology*.

"Thanks," B whispered. She pulled open the drawer marked T-U. The gray vapor poured out and formed a cloud. The woman's face inside was round and beaming, creased with smile lines.

"Another young researcher," the face said.

"Um, yes," B said. "May I have 'Using Ample Scolding'?"

"Splendid!" the face cried. "Wait right over there, dear, while I snag it for you."

In moments, the dragon-scale green book was in her hands. B hurried over to a study table and opened it. The binding creaked, and a marvelous ink-and-paper smell filled her nose as she pored over the beautifully illustrated pages, handwritten in meticulous calligraphy.

The book felt magical in her hands. Well, of course it was magical! But more than that, its smooth leather binding, the heft of each lustrous page, all seemed to reassure B. Here she'd find her answer! If anything could help her cure George of his zebra malady, she was sure it was this book.

She scanned through the table of contents, the page numbers overlaid with gold leaf. She scanned the section headings: Potion Antidotes, Reversing Overactive Love Potions, Undoing Jinxes and Hexes, Halting Magical Mayhem. Hmm, she should come back some time to study that last one. But there it was, the section she needed, last of all: Reversing Transformation Spells, followed by a long list of animals. Nothing about people! Oh, no!

In despair, B flipped to page 492, Monkeys and Other Primates, scanned through the chapter, and began to read:

There should be no need to mention reversing transforming spells cast on humans, because all well-trained witches understand how foolish it is to attempt such unruly magic. The effects can be permanent and irreversible. Any witches who accidentally cast transformation spells on humans should report immediately to the High Council of the Magical Rhyming Society. An emergency meeting of the High Council can be called if needed. Only the most highly qualified witches should devise an appropriate solution to the crisis before disaster strikes and the witching community is exposed to the entire world.

B's face fell forward until her forehead rested on the book pages. She could hear her heartbeat pounding in her ears.

She was doomed.

Chapter 13

Just in front of the table where B was sitting, two witches walked past, whispering about something. B just picked up the words, ". . . taken completely to pieces."

They could have been talking about anything, but B gulped. The thought of facing the Dismantle Squad was too much for her. She had to try one more thing before she confessed.

B flipped back to the table of contents. She scanned the list of chapters with her finger.

Chapter Seven, under Reversing Transformation Spells, was Wild Jungle Beasts. She quickly flipped to page 473 and scanned through the chapter. Several rhyming couplet possibilities were listed to reverse a botched animal transformation spell. The rhymes wouldn't do B any good; she had to spell her spells. B rested her chin on her fists, despondent. Probably all of the books in this library were written for rhyming witches. Was it the fact that she was a spelling witch that made all her spells turn out wonky?

The giant clock above the double doors chimed the quarter hour. Instead of a cuckoo bird popping out a door to do the honors, a magical mechanical peacock popped out and silently fanned its tail feathers.

Dawn would be back soon, so B would have to hurry.

The other remedies in the book seemed to suggest things B had already tried, such as trying an "undo" rhyme (she'd spelled it) or using a couplet to try to reset the animal's species.

She kept reading and came across a section written in strange, old-fashioned language with some words spelled oddly. It wasn't easy to make sense of it:

A Remedie for Failing Animal Reversals . . .

> *To reverse the spell and undo*
> *Get one from the original the brew*
> *And hair of the beast that troubles you.*

B blinked. "One from the original the brew"? She didn't know what that meant, but at least the fix didn't seem to involve a rhyme. Just a hair.

"Whatcha reading, B?"

B closed the book quickly and stood up. "Hey, Dawn, you all set to go?"

Her sister peered behind B's back to look at the table. "Yeah, we can leave. *Undoing Magic Spells?* What's the matter? Did you break a vase or something?"

B laughed — maybe a little too loudly. "Of course not. C'mon, let's go, it's probably dinnertime."

Dawn showed B where to return her book. A shower of sparkles swooped up the volume and returned it to its shelf.

As Dawn whisked them back home, B chanted the words of the strange rhyme in her head. *Get one from the original the brew and hair of the beast that troubles you.* It was like a puzzle she had to unravel.

The next morning, George wasn't on the bus. B's imagination conjured up the worst. Had her spell taken on a life of its own? Had his arms turned into forelegs, his hands and feet turned to hooves? B pictured George's mother fainting at the sight of her transformed son, then rushing her zebra-boy to the hospital in an ambulance . . . a newspaper reporter in the emergency room, snapping a photo . . . and the Dismantle Squad reading the next day's paper.

Stop it, B told herself sternly. *He probably overslept.*

In the foyer of the school, B took her latest Spirit Week addition — a plastic tiger nose that attached with an elastic strap — out of her bag and put it on while watching anxiously for George. Some kids had whiskers painted on their faces, others wore headbands with fuzzy orange ears. It was Tiger Day, since tigers were the school mascot.

"Nice nose, B!" Lisa Donahue called, passing by. B waved to her, then turned back to the window, relieved to see George galloping across the elementary school playground toward their school. In spite of her worry, B whistled in amazement. Look at him *move*! He was faster than a boy should be. With that kind of speed and power, there would be no stopping him on the soccer field.

Then she remembered, if the spell was getting stronger, it could be becoming more permanent. B was going to have to fix this — and fast.

He burst through the door, panting and sweaty.

"Where were you this morning?" B said. "I waited at the bus stop."

George stretched his long arms over his head. "Couldn't help it," he said. "Had to run. I just thought, why sit cooped up in a smelly old bus when I could feel the wind rippling through my mane?"

"You don't have a *mane*!" B hissed, glancing around to see if anyone had heard.

George laughed. "All right, my hair. It's just an expression."

B didn't think it was funny.

George's tail twitched out from behind his jeans. "Your tail," B whispered. "It's stripy orange!"

"Yep," George said proudly. "I washed off the charcoal dust and colored in the white fur with an orange marker. All this Spirit Week stuff is working out perfectly for me."

B shook her head. The risks were so huge! How could George be so relaxed about it?

He patted her shoulder. "I know you're worried," he said. "I'll be careful. But it hasn't been all bad, you know. I have so much energy! On the soccer field, I'm totally relaxed. I know I'm the fastest so I don't worry that the other guy's gonna get to the ball before me. I know I've got the strongest kick so their goalies don't worry me. I'm a brand-new player!"

"Brand-new *species*, you mean," B muttered.

The bell rang, and she left George and headed off to homeroom, thinking hard. She had to unravel that rhyme, and fast.

When she got to English class, she sat next to George as usual and sniffed the air.

"You need a shower," she told her friend.

"Sorry." He grinned. "I did shower this morning. It's all the running getting me sweaty. You should smell my socks. . . ."

"Ugh!" She laughed in spite of herself. "Sometimes you are so gross, George!"

"Got my soccer socks on today," he said, hitching up his pant leg to show her. "The whole team's been wearing their game socks all week for good luck."

"Pee-yew," she said, shaking her head. Then the sight of the sock made her stop still.

One from the original the brew.

The original brew that started all this trouble in the first place!

"George," she whispered urgently, "I need one of those socks."

"Huh?" He made a face at her. "At this point, they're practically hazardous waste. Even my mom won't touch 'em."

B reached into her backpack and pulled a zippered baggie from her lunch bag. Her mom had filled it with grapes for a snack. B gobbled up the grapes, then handed George the bag. "Sock, in bag, quick, before Mr. Bishop gets here."

George pried off one sneaker, grimacing at B. "I've got a feeling I'm not going to like this. Can't it wait until after tomorrow's game?"

"Not a chance," B said.

Just then Mr. Bishop came in. "Morning, class," he said. "Let's all settle down for this week's pop quiz."

After a few groans, the room went silent as Mr. Bishop passed out the papers. George slipped B the sock-in-a-bag, then tackled his quiz. It was on poetry terms — easy stuff for B.

She was halfway done when an earsplitting noise shattered the silence.

"Nee-hee-hee-hee!"

It was George, whinnying like a stallion!

After an astonished second of silence, the class burst out laughing. Mr. Bishop appeared by George's desk, twirling the point of his beard. B felt her face grow hot.

"I'm at a loss, George, to explain the sound

you just made," Mr. Bishop said. "Can you enlighten me?"

George bit his lip and grinned. "Well, the test question was on onomatopoeia. I was just . . . thinking about what that means, and I . . . thought about horses and I . . . forgot I was in public for a minute."

Mr. Bishop shook his head and chuckled. "Well, try to remember next time. And maybe, if you need to think of something, think of fish or mice, okay?"

"Okay."

B rolled her eyes. Nice save, George. A little close for comfort, but no goalie could do better. Still, this was a definite sign of "intensification."

Half of B's mind worked on the quiz, while the other half thought about the spell some more. One from the original brew, *check*. Hair of the beast that's troubling you?

That could only mean a zebra hair, right? But where was she get going to get zebra hair from?

They passed in their quizzes, then B handed George a note. "After school, we're going to the zoo."

Chapter 14

The zoo was across town, miles away, and B knew her mom wouldn't want her to ride the public transportation buses there all by herself. She'd need someone older to take her and George.

It was time to cash in some sister favors.

B knew that during lunch period, Dawn would be in the band room, practicing with the jazz ensemble. A few minutes before lunch ended, she left the cafeteria and headed down the corridors for the music wing. She camped outside the band room door and waited, glad she didn't have to chase down a human hamster in there again.

When the bell rang, Dawn came out, flanked by a handful of other tall teenagers carrying their band instruments in black cases. Dawn paused in her tracks at the sight of B. Her eyebrows rose slightly. It was code for, "Is everything okay?"

B nodded, then beckoned for Dawn to meet her away from the group.

"Catch up to you guys in a minute," Dawn said, breaking away from her group. "What's up?"

"I need a favor," B said in her sweetest, most pleading voice. "George and I need to go to the zoo today after school. It's important. Can you take us? Please?"

Dawn frowned. "The zoo? Why today? What's the big rush?"

"Oh, it's a project," B said vaguely. "I'm writing a research paper on zebras and I want to, um, observe real ones, and . . . take some pictures of them." B blushed. *It's true. I am writing a research paper on zebras! I just need to remember to bring the camera.*

"I was going to get together with the girls this afternoon," Dawn said. "You remember Angela, Stef, and Macey?"

B remembered them all right. They were witches

from Dawn's magic class and the ones who first showed B what a bag-cauldron could do.

"Why don't they come, too?" B said. "I've got enough allowance saved to treat you all to ice cream sundaes at the zoo. Deal?"

Dawn shrugged. "I'll check with them. They probably won't mind. We'll leave from home at four, after my softball practice."

B gave Dawn a quick hug. "Thank you *soooo* much!"

"Ack, you poked me with your tiger nose!"

"Sorry."

At four o'clock, George and B were waiting on B's front porch for Dawn to be ready and her friends to arrive. At B's insistence, George had stuffed his tail down a leg of his jeans. Nightshade, B's black cat, twined himself in and out between B's ankles, and she scratched him absentmindedly between his ears.

Dawn's friends came into view, walking around the corner — Angela, with sleek black hair and a shiny black leather jacket; Stef, with spiky hair dyed pink today, and wearing a rainbow-striped vest and purple high-top sneakers; and Macey, whose long red hair was braided. B suspected some magical needlework had gone into her pretty hand-knit sweater.

"Hey, B," Macey said. "We haven't seen you in a while! Thanks for inviting us to come to the zoo with you."

"Yeah, thanks for the ice cream," Stef said. "Make mine a triple-fudge caramel banana split."

"All I want is a diet soda," said Angela, checking her reflection in a handheld mirror.

"Everyone, this is George, my best friend," B said. "George, this is Angela, and Stef, and Macey."

"Hey," George said, turning a little red when he shook hands with Macey. B looked at him sideways, suppressing a smile.

"What kind of ice cream are you getting, George?" Macey asked.

"Oh, uh, I, er, Coach says not much sweets, I mean, I . . . think I'll just have a salad." His last words tumbled out awkwardly. Stef threw back her head and hooted with laughter. "A *salad*? Since when does a kid pick salad over a sundae?"

"He's just a little health conscious before the big game," B said, not wanting them to think too much about it.

Just then, Dawn opened the front door, freshly showered and beautified. "Hey, girls!" she cried, hugging all her friends.

"C'mon, let's hurry or we'll have to wait for another bus." They all walked to the bus stop. After twenty minutes and a transfer, they reached the zoo and paid their entry fees.

"Let's go see the zebras first," B told George and the older girls. "Then we can get that out of the way and get the ice cream."

"What's your hurry?" Stef said. "I want to see the penguins. Waddle, waddle." She pretended to walk like a penguin.

Macey sidled up to B. "Hon, what's your little friend up to?"

B turned to see George bending low over some shrubbery, taking a big bite out of a leafy branch. "Oh, he's always clowning around," B said, then grabbed George and stepped on his toe. "Watch it, zebra-boy," she whispered. "No grazing, okay?"

"But it smells so good!" George protested. "Don't you want a bite, too?"

"No, and neither do you," B said. "I brought some chocolate; want some?"

George stuck out his tongue. "Yick. No thanks." B blinked. Was it just her imagination, or had George's tongue gotten really long all of a sudden?

She steered George toward the penguin house, following the older girls. After the penguins they toured the aquarium, the reptile house, and then the aviary. George seemed bored, and B, who ordinarily loved the zoo, was anxious. She was in no mood to marvel at parrots or pythons. Zebras were her only research interest today.

At last she persuaded Dawn and her friends to join them for the African safari train ride. They climbed aboard and waited for the train car to fill. George bounced up and down on his seat and let loose another zebra whinny. Dawn and her friends sat halfway across the train and avoided looking at him.

The train car was three-quarters full when a young man in a zoo T-shirt got on board. "Hi, folks," he said. "I'm Mack, and I'll be your safari guide today. I'm a junior at Springfield State College, majoring in zoology."

B noticed Dawn sit up a little straighter, and Angela adjust her hair.

"The most important safety rule today is to stay in your seats, and don't, under any circumstances, attempt to open the door of the train car, okay? Remember, they look fascinating, but these are wild animals we're dealing with. We don't want anybody hurt — not the animals, and not you folks. Okay, everyone ready? Here we go."

The train lurched forward. At first B saw nothing but trees.

"Giraffes!" a little girl cried.

Mack described the zoo's giraffe families, including the two calves that had been born there that year, as the train chugged forward. B watched the giraffes eat leaves off the treetops until the train turned a corner and passed through another gate.

"There's a special kind of animal in this enclosure," Mack said. "Sometimes we don't see them if they're resting. Can anyone guess what's in here?"

B scanned the grassy landscape, looking for black and white stripes. Out of the corner of her eye she saw a tawny flash of fur.

"LION!" George screamed. "RUN!" He raced down the aisle of the train car and climbed onto the rear seat, whinnying in terror.

"Whoa, buddy!" Mack cried. "It's okay; you're safe inside the train!"

B caught a glimpse of a brown mane and a huge, lanky body loping across the enclosure. She hurried down the aisle to George and yanked his arm till he sat down with a thud. Other zoo visitors shot disapproving glances at them, and Dawn sent B a *what-on-earth-is-going-on* look. B patted George's shoulder until he settled down.

The train left the lion enclosure and entered the elephant area. The occupants of the train ran to the windows, *ooh*ing and *aah*ing about the baby elephants, and B sighed with relief as the focus shifted off the backseat.

"You okay, George?"

"I think so," George panted. "Did you see the size of that guy? He could have eaten me for lunch!"

"Well, he didn't," B said.

"Look, zebras!" the same little girl cried. The train had entered another gated area.

B's heartbeat raced. This was the moment. But here she was, stuck inside a train! How was she ever going to get her hands on a zebra hair? Could magic help? To be so close, and still not get a hair . . .

She could see the zebras now, some running through the field, others grazing placidly. They were beautiful, she had to admit, but all she could think about were those millions of zebra hairs, just out of reach!

George pressed his nose against the glass. "Look at 'em, B! Have you ever seen something so amazing?"

"Well, um . . ." B didn't have time to finish. George clambered over her, unbolted the rear emergency exit door, and jumped off the train!

Chapter 15

The emergency alarm shrilled.

Brakes hissed as the train came to a stop.

"Get back here, kid!" Mack cried. He whipped out a walkie-talkie. "Security, we have a situation in the zebra pen. Send a coupla guys, pronto!"

B watched George's back, racing off toward the zebras, then looked at Dawn and her friends, whose mouths were still hanging open in shock.

What could she do? The only way out of this mess was to get a zebra hair!

B leaped through the door and followed George.

"Come back here!" Mack hollered.

B sprinted through the tall grass. George was well ahead of her, and pulling farther away. *I couldn't catch George even if he wasn't a zebra,* B thought, *but I have to try.*

The zebras, grazing in groups, looked like a stripy optical illusion in the distance. One of them raised its head, ears pricked, and soon the whole herd was alert, hearing George's footsteps approaching.

"Hey, you kids! Stop this *instant* and come back to the train!"

B glanced over her shoulder to see Mack and another zoo worker racing after them.

Uh-oh.

The zebras broke off their grazing and galloped around the perimeter of the pen in long, graceful strides, their black tails streaming. George swerved to follow them, his long legs flying. A pair of elephants, watching from over the fence, trumpeted at all the excitement.

"Forget the girl, get that crazy boy!" Mack called to his comrade. The zoo workers passed B and closed in on George. He ran in a zigzag, just like the zebras were doing. He let out a loud whinny, and a few of the younger zebras paused and turned to look back at him.

There was no way she could catch up to George now, so B paused to catch her breath. It was all she could do not to flop in the grass.

Then she saw them, not far off, hiding behind a thicket of bushes — a mother zebra and her calf, who had ducked underneath her round belly. The mother zebra watched the commotion warily.

B tried to still her breath so the zebras wouldn't be startled. She stared at them through the leafy cover.

For a second B forgot everything else. The zebra was magnificent! Her muscles rippled under her smooth hide, and the stark black and white of her stripes was dazzling. Her mane stood stiff and upright, as B had learned from her zebra research. But to see one here, so close, breathing, watching, and nuzzling her calf, made all the online photographs insignificant by comparison.

"H-A-I-R," B whispered, hoping not to scare the mother zebra away.

Her pointy ears twitched, but she didn't run. Something *twinged* on the top of her mane, and a stiff black hair floated into B's outstretched hand.

"Gotcha!" the security guards cried, and B turned just in time to see Mack nail George with a perfect football tackle. Gripping the hair tightly, she hurried over to see if her best friend was okay.

He was. He'd landed in a cushy spot: the soft mud around the zebras' drinking hole.

"I have never been so embarrassed in my life," Angela declared on the bus back home. "Next time your sister wants us to take her somewhere, Dawn, will you please make sure she leaves her immature friends at home?"

B avoided Dawn's glare.

"We won't be taking either of them to the zoo any time soon," Stef said, "since they've both been *banned for a year*!"

"They don't need to rub our noses in it," George

muttered to B. The mud on his face and shirt was slowly forming a crust.

B bit her lip. She couldn't exactly defend George for what he'd done, and yet, she was as much to blame for turning him half zebra in the first place.

"I'm just bummed that they wouldn't even let us stay long enough to buy ice cream," Macey said. "You owe us, B."

B nodded. Ice cream was the least of her worries. What would her parents say when they heard about this? More important, would the concoction fix George?

Dawn glared at B. B could feel a lecture coming on. Sure enough, "B, I suppose you thought you were helping," Dawn said, "but that was so ridiculous of you to go chasing after George. The zebras could have trampled you to death! What if George had spooked them, and they'd stampeded?"

"Look at the bright side," Macey said. "At least he chased after zebras, not alligators."

"The only bright side is that it's over," Dawn said. "Let's get the kids home, then go uptown to the

Magical Moo. I think we all need to unwind. My treat."

Dawn turned and shot B a raised-eyebrow look. The look was sister-code for, "You're gonna pay me back for the ice cream tonight."

B nodded. Fair enough.

At the bus stop, the girls headed uptown while George and B headed for home.

"I don't know what came over me back there, B," George said. "I'm sorry I got you into trouble."

B sighed. "Don't be sorry, George," she said. "I'm the one that got you into trouble, really."

"Yeah, but I persuaded you to do it in the first place," George said.

"So that makes us even. But listen, I've got . . . an idea." She caught herself on the brink of saying, "A zebra hair!" She reached into her jacket pocket and pulled out the bagged stinky soccer sock and the tissue she'd wrapped the zebra hair in. *One from the original the brew, and hair of the beast that troubles you. I've got them both.*

But what should she spell? To reverse the spell and undo . . .

She closed her eyes. "R-E-V-E-R-S-E."

She opened them and . . . *oh, no!*

"Still got the tail; I can tell," George said. Then he saw B. "What's the matter?" he cried, panic in his voice.

B pointed a shaky finger at him. "Your face!"

George rubbed furiously at his cheeks. "What, the mud?"

"Nope," B said, putting a hand over her eyes. "You've got more zebra stripes."

Chapter 16

B didn't even look for George at the bus the next morning. She knew he'd be galloping to school, and she knew there was no way to hide the stripes. With each street the bus turned down, B felt disaster coming closer. She was in over her head; she had meddled with magic too advanced for her, and she knew she had to confess to Mr. Bishop. She couldn't get out of this without his help. And she couldn't let her friend be transformed into a zebra permanently.

B dragged herself to her locker and through homeroom. "Did you see what George did this morning?" Jamal Burns said to B on the way to

English. "He's brave, man. He painted himself with tiger stripes for the big game."

"He . . . he did?" B tried to pretend she didn't know. "Orange and black, like a tiger?"

"He only painted the black ones. But it's all over him. The rest of the team is jealous that he thought of it."

"That George," B said, pretending to laugh. "He's always thinking up something." Leaving Jamal behind, B plowed her way through the halls, racing to English to be on the scene when Mr. Bishop first laid eyes on her friend.

She found George all decked out in his team jersey and shorts, showing his arms, legs, neck, and face plastered with black zebra stripes. His tail was in plain view today, but no one seemed to pay attention to it, perhaps because he'd been wearing it nearly all week. His teammates were high-fiving him and examining his stripes admiringly.

"My mom would never let me do that."

"I heard they were tattoos."

"Don't be an idiot!"

"You did your back, too? You're crazy!"

George beamed at B. "I love my stripes," he said. "This is the best Spirit Week costume ever."

B sighed. She leaned over to George and whispered, "I'm turning myself in."

"Aw, come on," he said. "Can't you wait till after the game? I'm gonna play like crazy today. I can just feel it. Did you see how fast I was running yesterday at the zoo?"

"Don't remind me," B said. "Personally, I might need a lifetime to forget yesterday at the zoo."

"But I need to be the Zebra to help us win the game!" George pleaded.

Before B could respond, Mr. Bishop came into the room and class began. B watched her teacher like a hawk for any sign of special attention paid to George, curiosity, *anything*. But her magical English teacher seemed just like his usual cheerful self. He was decked out in school colors like everyone else, and wearing a cap with a huge tiger mascot made of foam rubber on top. He even complimented George on his school spirit, all without any sign of concern.

When class ended, George stood up to leave, but B grabbed his arm.

"We're ending this now," she whispered. She felt bad about disappointing George, but it was time to fix this.

The other students had filed out, and B practically dragged George to Mr. Bishop's desk.

"Ready for the big game?" Mr. Bishop asked George.

"I sure am," George said. "I'm more ready than I've ever been."

B's heart started thumping and she wanted to bolt out of the room, but she forced herself to stay. Dismantle Squad or no, she was going to have to face the consequences of her magic. "We really need your help, Mr. Bishop."

Mr. Bishop sat up. "Anything you need, B."

She was going to do it — confess that she had told George about her magic, that she had turned him into a zebra, and that she'd been hiding it for days — but in the long pause, George interrupted her.

"B and I really want you to come to the game and cheer on the team," George declared, nudging B hard.

B stared at her best friend.

Mr. Bishop smiled. "Of course! I've got to support my students and my school, right? I'll be there."

"Great!" George said, grabbing B's arm and pulling her away. "Gotta get to lunch now. I need my carbs."

In the hallway, George whispered, "Come on, B. Just let me have a couple more hours and then you can confess."

B sighed. If she had left it too late and the spell was actually permanent, it would be the least she could do to let George have his moment of glory as a superathlete.

"Okay," she agreed.

George let out an excited whinny and galloped off.

B followed slowly, brooding.

Would she lose her magic forever? Would she be

banned from the witching community? What would happen to George?

Had too much time passed since the first spell was cast? Would he remain a zebra-boy forever? Stripes today, forelegs tomorrow. That was probably how it would go.

He wouldn't be able to live at home anymore — they'd put him in the zoo. The zoo that B was banned from visiting!

She ate her lunch like it was her last meal.

After school, B went outside and climbed to the far end of the topmost bleacher to wait for the soccer game to start. She was too upset to want to talk to anyone.

The referees in their black-and-white striped jerseys ran out onto the field. B winced at the sight. Zebras everywhere!

Then the home team ran out to the loud beat of their warm-up song. They waved to the crowd in the rapidly filling bleachers, then each player pounded a ball into an unguarded goal. The junior cheerleaders squealed when George, as team captain, kicked the last ball in.

"Gooooooooo, TIGERS!" the cheerleaders screamed. "Gimme a T! Gimme an I! Gimme a G!"

B was almost glad she didn't feel like cheering. Those cheerleaders nearly tricked her into turning the whole squad into preteen tigresses. Pretty soon she'd have her own zoo, right here at the school.

Just then, Mr. Bishop climbed up the bleacher steps and sat next to another teacher, still wearing his crazy tiger cap. B felt her body stiffen at the sight of him.

No more magic lessons. No more magic, period.

It was the price she had to pay.

The whistle blew, and the game began. The home team Tigers, in their orange jerseys, played the neighboring Falcons, in blue. It wasn't hard to spot George in the crowd — his height made him different enough, not to mention the stripes all over his body.

But what was he doing out there? A teammate sent him a perfect pass, with an open shot at the goal, and instead of seizing the opportunity, George ignored the pass and ran in crazy circles around the defensive players from the other team. They punted the ball thirty yards back down the field, and the home team fans groaned.

"C'mon, George," B said under her breath. "You wanted zebra abilities for this game. You have to use them!"

Coach Lyons rose from the bench and hollered, "Quit clowning around, George!" While the rest of the Tiger team had retreated back to play defense, George had gone down on all fours, sniffing a tuft of grass and taking a bite out of it.

"What's George *doing*?" some kids near B were saying. "Isn't he the captain?"

Just then the whistle blew. While B was watching George, the Falcons had scored a goal!

It was painful to watch. George couldn't seem to pay attention to soccer when there was grass underfoot. Coach Lyons gave him one more chance, but the Falcons scored a second goal, and the Tigers coach benched his captain. A couple of kids booed.

B sat with her chin in her hands. The second

twenty minutes began, and the Tigers did their best without George. This was what he'd had been afraid of — getting benched. Oddly enough, he didn't seem to care. He was crawling under the bench, nosing the grass.

George, you're making me crazy!

Then she blinked.

Making me crazy. Troubling me.

The hair of the beast that's troubling you!

What if the animal transformation reversal spell wasn't talking about a hair from the *type* of animal, but hair from the actual animal whose transformation had gone wrong?

In other words, a hair from George?

Chapter 17

B rose in the stands and hurried down the steps. She still had the stinky sock and zebra hair stuffed into the bottom of her backpack, so she could do the spell again.

With George sitting right there on the bench, it shouldn't be hard to snag a hair. But before B could reach him, Coach Lyons signaled the ref for a substitution. The other center forward had slipped and twisted his ankle.

"No more shenanigans, George," B heard the coach tell her friend. "You've got to turn this game around. Play like you've been playing in practice all week!"

And he was gone. B slumped down into a seat on the front row, thinking hard. How could she reach George? She didn't dare attempt a summoning spell for a piece of George's hair, from so far away across the field. Someone might see the magic or she could summon the wrong thing entirely.

Finally, the whistle blew for halftime. The players, flushed in the face, were trotting back to the bench. The score was still at 2–0.

B slipped into the row right behind where the team would sit, hoping that George would sit down and she'd be able to snag a hair. But they didn't sit. Coach Lyons kept them in a huddle for a long time. When it finally broke up, everyone went for water. George guzzled about a quart of it.

B waved to him, called to him, tried to catch his eye, but her best friend never seemed to notice. It seemed that all he could think of was grazing. . . .

Grazing!

B ran around behind the bleachers and slipped through the metal slats until she was underneath. Here, where the grass grew thick and unmowed, B found a huge juicy patch of dandelion greens that she scooped up. Then she ran back out to where George stood with his teammates, and called to him.

This time, he turned.

She waved the fistful of greens like she was beckoning to a horse. And George trotted over just as a horse would have.

"Awesome!" he cried, reaching for the greens. "I needed an energy boost, but all they have over there is oranges. Yick!"

B glanced over her shoulder toward where Mr. Bishop was. "Careful," she whispered to George. "Don't let people see you eating weeds!"

But George buried his face in the fresh-picked salad. B could only hope no one saw him doing it. She leaned forward, grabbed a couple of his shaggy blond hairs, and yanked them out.

"Ow!"

"Whoops, sorry," B said, trying to sound innocent. "Have some more dandelions."

He hadn't gotten far before the warning whistle blew, and he galloped off to rejoin the game. B crept back under the bleachers where she could hide. She pulled out the stinky sock once more and held it in one outstretched hand, with George's hair in the other. She closed her eyes and thought about George, his ears, his tail, his stripes. This had to work. It *had to.*

"U-N-D-O," she spelled.

The whistle blew to kick off the second half. B climbed out from underneath the bleachers and resumed her seat on the top row, watching George intently. Were his stripes fading? She couldn't tell. He did seem to be standing taller, though, and he was definitely more focused on the game. In fact, his footwork was outstanding! Twice he completely buffaloed a Falcon defender and got past him easily.

"GO, GEORGE!" The crowd was noticing a difference as well. "GO, GEORGE!" they yelled.

B joined in the cheer, but kept her eyes glued on her friend. He swept past the bleachers, and B squinted. The stripes were less noticeable now. She was 99 percent sure of it.

A Tiger defender sent a long pass sailing down

the field, and George was there to meet it. He passed to a teammate, who dodged a Falcon and sent it back to George. George put it in the net!

The Tiger bleachers went berserk. B almost wished she had her pom-poms.

The whistle blew, and the game resumed.

No doubt anymore — none whatsoever. Those stripes were on their way out. Relief flooded over B. She cheered herself hoarse.

With ten minutes left on the clock, George scored another goal to tie the score. Feet flashing, clock ticking, the Falcons and Tigers were dueling it out for the ball every second. B was on the edge of the bench, watching every move. George was having a great game, not as La Zebra, but as himself. With seconds left on the clock, he maneuvered a brilliant pass to Jamal Burns, who headed it into the goalie's net.

The whistle blew.

The Tigers had won!

Chapter 18

The Tigers swarmed George and Jamal and hoisted them up on their shoulders, cheering. The cheerleaders surrounded the team, and the fans in the bleachers surged onto the field. B had a feeling she might get laryngitis for a week, she was screaming so loud. Relief that the spell was over made her giddy, and to see her best friend play so well — without magical help — and win made her happiness complete.

She hurried down the bleachers to wait for George's feet to hit the ground. She had to wait for Coach Lyons to put him in a headlock and give his scalp a noogie. Finally George broke away from the adoring masses and saw B. He ran to her and gave her a big hug.

"Did you see, B? Did you see how I played like La Zebra? I don't ever want you to switch me back. I don't care how weird I look. I have you to thank for this!"

B handed George a cup of energy drink she'd snagged from the team manager. "No, you don't, silly," she said. "Look at yourself."

George held up his arm and stared. "The stripes are gone!" He rubbed his skin.

B couldn't stop laughing.

George grabbed at his shorts. "And my tail is gone!"

B nodded. "Gone for good. You should sleep better now. No more hearing double."

"Oh, no!" George panicked. "Now I'll never play that well again!" He wiped his face with his jersey.

"It just so happens, George," B said, "that I turned you back before the second half began. All your good playing today was after I switched you. If you don't mind my saying so, as a zebra you were pretty lousy on the field. More interested in grazing than in scoring."

George seemed dazed. He twisted himself

around and swatted at his lower back, still searching for his zebra tail.

"Believe me, George, you won that game on talent and skill — and guts. You believed you were La Zebra, so you played like him. You can do that every week. And you don't need a tail to do it."

It took George a minute of scratching where his zebra ears had once been to really believe it was all true. Then he stood a bit taller. "Thanks, B. For trying to help, and for believing in me. How did you figure out a way to reverse the spell?"

"Magic," B said with a smile. "That's my secret."

B glanced over to where Mr. Bishop stood, talking with Coach Lyons. He turned slightly, met B's gaze, and winked.

Hmmm . . .

"Well, I knew you'd figure it out," George said. "I was never worried. Not really. I'll bet you're the best young witch in that whole M.R. whatever-it-is world you're always talking about."

"Ssshhh!" B said. "Ready to go?" she asked, heading out to the street behind the school. George fell into step beside her.

"No more transformations," said B. "And no more spells on humans!"

"*Nee-hee-hee!*" George whinnied.

B halted in her tracks.

George laughed. "Just kidding!"

B shook her head, then laughed with him. "Let's go home and get something to eat."

"I'll say," George said. "I've gone a whole week without chocolate!"

B's charmed adventures continue in

Read on for a sneak peek!

B's paintbrush hovered over the rough paper tacked to her easel. With the faintest of strokes, she trailed the tip of the bristles in a graceful arc.

Another whisker for Nightshade, her cat. Only about twenty more to go.

Beatrix, or "B" for short, glanced at the photo of her black tomcat pinned to the corner of the easel. She was so absorbed in her work that a voice at her shoulder made her jump.

"Quit your humming, Bumblebee," Jason Jameson said. "You sound like a beehive, and you're giving the rest of us a headache."

B glowered at Jason, who'd been a raging pest ever since preschool. Now that sixth grade was here, he was worse. He and his insect insults, reserved especially for B because of her nickname, drove her buggy.

"I thought everyone liked the Black Cats," B said, pretending to sound innocent.

"Was that 'Yowl' you were humming?" Jamal Burns asked.

"I bet that'll be the first song they play at

Saturday's show," Kim Silsby said. "I'm so jealous you've got tickets, B!"

B grinned. "Only because George won the spelling bee, and shared one of his tickets with me," she said. "I can barely wait until Saturday night."

"You're not the only one with tickets, Cockroach," Jason scoffed. "My parents bought me a seat in the second row. Betcha don't know how much that cost."

"Who cares what it cost? Quit showing off, Jason," Kim said.

B dipped her brush once more and carefully traced another whisker, and then another, peering at the photograph between strokes to get each one perfect.

She was on her second-to-last one when Miss Willow's voice made her jump, dragging her brush across Nightshade's face and smearing one of his amber-colored eyes.

"Everyone," her art teacher said in an extra-cheery voice, "I have an announcement to make."

B groaned silently. Her painting was ruined! Here was where a little spot of magic would come in handy. Checking quickly to see that no one was looking at her easel, B whispered, "E-R-A-S-E." The errant black stroke disappeared, as B had known it would—but so did all the whiskers she'd added that morning! B sighed. Typical of B's special brand of magic. When she spelled words, things happened, but not always the things she had in mind!

"Now, class," Miss Willow said, "I want you all to meet a new student in our school, just joining us today. Her name is Katrina Lang."

Next to Miss Willow's cluttered desk stood a shy-looking girl in a dark skirt and a cream-colored sweater, very trim and proper except for her dark hair pulled back into a messy bun.

"What a *nerd*!" Jason whispered to Jenny Springbranch, who tittered softly.

"Beatrix, will you show Katrina where the paints are kept? Katrina, we're painting animal portraits today."

"Her name may be *Kat*-rina," Jason whispered loudly to Jenny, "but she looks more like a mouse to me. Hey, *Kat*-rina!" His freckle-plastered face broke into a nasty grin. "Why doncha paint a mouse self-portrait?"

Katrina's jaw set in a hard line. B steered her toward the back counter where the paints were kept. "Don't pay any attention to him," B told Katrina. "Most people here are nice."

Katrina studied B's face for a minute, her dark green eyes wary and doubtful.

"Here, let's fill your paint tray," B said. "What animal are you going to paint?"

"A panther," Katrina said without hesitation.

"Excellent!" B said. "Here's the bottle of black."

"Thanks, Beatrix," Katrina said, this time with a warm smile.

"Not a problem. Call me 'B.' Most everyone does."

"Okay." Katrina grinned. "Call me 'Trina.'"

"Sounds good."

They returned to their workstations. Jason Jameson grabbed bottles of green and orange paint, squirted way too much of it into the tray on his easel, and bumped into B's easel accidentally-on-purpose after returning the bottles to the back counter.

Jason snickered and dipped his brush in the orange paint. "Stinkbug!" he said.

B fumed. She stared at Jason's paints. "S-P-I-L-L," she whispered under her breath.

Jason's easel pitched toward him. His paint tray flipped upside-down, landing on the legs of his pants before clattering to the floor.